W9-BYX-581

Praise for A WORK IN PROGRESS

"With gut-wrenching delicacy and heartfelt honesty, Jarrett Lerner skillfully pairs illustrations and verse to offer us a road map back to forgiveness and self-realization in a world that is often cruel and heartless to those it has cast out. Jarrett's book is a masterpiece of hope and resilience and will change the trajectory of its readers. For the boys who have longed to be seen, for the adults who have needed to see them, this book will save lives."
—Pernille Ripp, global educator, author, and creator of the Global Read Aloud

"Every kid that I have ever taught would find something for their hearts in A Work in Progress. This book truly is for EVERY reader."
—Colby Sharp, educator, author, and editor of The Creativity Project

"With deftness, depth, and care, Will's honest voice reels you into this vitally important page-turner with unassumingly casual ease. Will's raw vulnerability and hard-fought hope will be a conversation starter and life changer for readers of all ages."
—Shelley Johannes, author-illustrator of Beatrice Zinker, Upside Down Thinker

"I couldn't put this remarkable book down. Will's deeply moving journey toward treating himself with kindness is a powerful message for readers of all ages. I know this beautiful book is going to make a difference for so many, kids and grown-ups alike."
—Supriya Kelkar, author of American as Paneer Pie

Also by Jarrett Lerner

EngiNerds
Revenge of the EngiNerds
EngiNerds Strike Back

Geeger the Robot Goes to School
Geeger the Robot Lost and Found
Geeger the Robot to the Rescue
Geeger the Robot Party Pal
Geeger the Robot Goes for Gold

Give This Book a Title
Give This Book a Cover

The Hunger Heroes: Missed Meal Mayhem
The Hunger Heroes: Snack Cabinet Sabotage

Nat the Cat Takes a Nap
Nat the Cat Takes a Bath

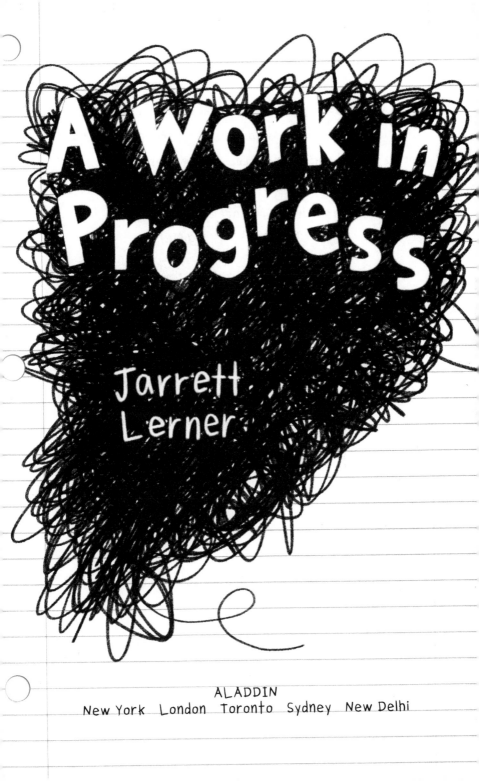

A Work in Progress

Jarrett
Lerner

ALADDIN
New York   London   Toronto   Sydney   New Delhi

CONTENT WARNING: This story contains content that may be triggering for some readers, including, but not limited to, depictions of body shaming, body dysmorphia, binge eating, food restriction, and disordered eating. Please be aware, read with care, and, if needed, refer to the resources listed on page 360.

ALADDIN
An imprint of Simon & Schuster Children's Publishing Division
1230 Avenue of the Americas, New York, New York 10020
First Aladdin hardcover edition May 2023
Text copyright © 2023 by Jarrett Lerner
Illustrations copyright © 2023 by Jarrett Lerner
All rights reserved, including the right of reproduction in whole or in part in any form.
ALADDIN and related logo are registered trademarks of Simon & Schuster, Inc.
For information about special discounts for bulk purchases, please contact Simon & Schuster Special Sales at 1-866-506-1949 or business@simonandschuster.com.
The Simon & Schuster Speakers Bureau can bring authors to your live event. For more information or to book an event contact the Simon & Schuster Speakers Bureau at 1-866-248-3049 or visit our website at www.simonspeakers.com.
Designed by Heather Palisi
The illustrations for this book were rendered digitally.
The text of this book was set in A Font in Progress.
Manufactured in the United States of America 0523 BVG
10 9 8 7 6 5 4
Library of Congress Control Number 2022936641
ISBN 9781665905152
ISBN 9781665905176 (ebook)

For anyone
who has ever felt
less than

I always
think back
to fourth grade . . .

I was minding my business
hanging out
in the hallway
with Dave
and Andrew
and Devin
when I felt a tap
on my shoulder.

I turned around
and saw a kid—

    Nick Fisher

—standing there.

Nick was in my grade
and small for his age.
In fourth grade
he looked more like
a third grader
or even
a second grader.

And I don't know
if it was because of that
or because of something else
he had going on
in his life
but he always went around
already halfway
to angry.
He was the kind of kid
who'd snap at you
for no reason
if you just looked at him
the wrong way
on the wrong day.

All of which is why
I was kind of worried
when I turned around
and saw it was Nick
who'd tapped me.
That
and the fact
that he was already

scowling.

I knew
right then
that whatever his reason
for getting my attention—

it couldn't
be good.

"You're **FAT**," Nick said.

No no no—

he **SPAT** it.

That word. Nick

He spat it at me
like it was the worst one
he knew.

Like I'd committed
a crime
and he wanted
to make sure
I knew
I was **GUILTY**.

"You're **FAT**," Nick said
and the whole entire hallway
fell silent.
Everyone
was looking.
Everyone
was listening.

And then
he said it
again:

"You're **FAT**.
And **EVERYONE**
thinks it."

At first
I was too stunned
to do
a thing.
My brain
was racing.
My heart
pounding.
But the rest
of me?
Frozen
stiff.
All I
could do
was stare
at the shark
showing off
its teeth
on Nick's
T-shirt.

Then Dave—
he set his hand
on my shoulder
and whispered,

"Will,"

and for whatever reason
that broke
the spell.

And then
I got out of there
as fast
as I could.

I fled.

FAT!

Something like that happens to you—

something like what happened to me
in that hallway
with Nick Fisher
in fourth grade

—and it never
leaves
your head.

It's in there.

For   ever.

PERMANENTLY.

The memory
might as well
be tattooed
on your brain.

It'll replay
again and again
and again
and
again.

On bad days
of course.

But on good days
too.

On days
that **HAD** been
good.

Until . . .

BAM!

It sneaks up
on you.
It just   **POPS OUT**
        out of
the blue.

And it's not long before
you don't even need
the Nick Fishers of the world
to be there
to tell you
what they think
of you—
what the whole entire world thinks
of you—
that you
are less than
you
are inferior
you
are an animal
not worthy
of kindness
or consideration
or respect.

Soon enough

you take care
of saying all that
for them.

You start thinking
just like they do.

You start hurling
the insults
at yourself.

You become
your own
bully.

And you do the job better
than anyone else
possibly
could.

I hid.

That day
after Nick said what he said
I hurried out of sight
barreled into the first bathroom
I came across
and locked myself
in a stall.

I ran   away

          and
hid.

I sat there—

          in that cramped
          stinking stall
          on the gross
          dirty toilet

—and tried
and failed
and   tried
and failed
to catch my

breath and
keep the tears
from pouring out
and drowning
me.

Dave
and Andrew
and Devin
found me
eventually.
And they said
all the right things.
Or maybe not
the **RIGHT** things—
but all the things
right then
that I wanted
to hear.

They called Nick
a jerk.
An idiot.
A loser.
They made a bunch of jokes
about how short he was.

And little by little
it cheered me up.
Even though
a part of me
didn't **WANT** to be
cheered up.

Finally
I unlocked the door.
Stepped out
of the stall.

My friends
looked happy.
They looked
RELIEVED.
Devin smiled.
Andrew grinned.
Dave gave me
a fist bump
and grabbed my shoulders
for a squeeze.
And I knew
right away
that they thought
it was over.
That the whole

ugly incident
with Nick
could already be
put behind us.
We could move on
get back
to our regularly scheduled lives—
which did **NOT** include
anything
as serious
or dramatic
as all that had happened
that day.

And
        I went with it.

Standing there
in the bathroom
with my smiling
happy friends
I decided
to pretend
that all that
was true.

        Why?

I didn't
really understand it
then.
But I get it
now.
In that moment
I felt like I
should be thankful
that Dave and Andrew and Devin
had gone through the trouble
of finding me
of cheering me up.
Like I
should be thankful
that they still wanted
to be friends
with me.
ME.
A fat kid
who everyone thought
was fat
and less than.
I felt
all of a sudden
like they had been
and were now
doing me a favor

by letting **ME**
be friends with them
EVEN THOUGH
I was fat.
And I felt
like I was now
on borrowed time.
Like if I
was a downer
about all this—

if
instead of smiling
along with them
I broke down
like I wanted to
and cried

—they'd decide
it wasn't worth it.
They'd stop being
so generous
and kind.
They'd cut me out
of their lives
right that very second
and then I wouldn't just

be fat—
I'd be fat
AND friendless
which back then
I was pretty sure
was the only thing
worse.

So I wiped away
my tears.

I mopped up
my snot.

I put on a smile—
and instead
of hiding
in bathrooms
I learned
how to hide
in plain sight.

I've always been

big.

Bigger

than everyone else.

And it's not like
I never noticed.
Of course
I noticed.
Of course
I already knew.

But up until that point—

    till that moment
    in that hallway
    with Nick Fisher

—I hadn't known
my size mattered.
I hadn't known
it was the thing
about me
that mattered most
to the rest
of the world.
I hadn't known
that it made everyone
who saw me
feel uncomfortable
or filled them
with disgust.

And **THAT**
was what Nick
was really telling me
that day.
With his angry face.
With his raised shoulders.
With the way
he **SPAT**
that word
at me.

FAT.

For years
I'd been living
my life
like I was
as good
as anyone else.
Like I could act
like everyone else—

wearing whatever clothes
I wanted
eating my lunch
in public
raising my hand

in class
expecting
other people
not to sneer
or chuckle
or crack
a joke
every time
they passed me
in the hallway
or saw me
step into
a room.

And Nick
had let me know
I was wrong.

Wrong
wrong
wrong
wrong
WRONG.

And my friends?
The ones
who'd come

and found me
in the bathroom . . .

They didn't argue
with that.

They **COULDN'T** argue
with that.

And I can't
blame them.
They were in
the fourth grade.
So was I.
And as soon as
I realized
my size mattered
so much
to everyone else
it mattered
that much
to me.
What Nick said
was now
as factual to me
as anything.

Grass   is green.

The sky   is blue.

You   are fat

           and
               therefore

you   are less than.

As weird
as it sounds—
sometimes
I'm grateful
for Nick.

He opened
my eyes.

Until he said
what he said
I hadn't known
how other people
saw me.

I'd been
oblivious.
FAT
and oblivious.

It was so . . .

      embarrassing.

But now—
thanks to Nick—
I saw it too.

That night—

    the night
    of the day
    that Nick Fisher
    opened my eyes
    in that hallway

—I went through
all my clothes.

My drawers.

My closet.

I yanked
at the necks
of my T-shirts
and spilled soda
all over
my sweatshirts
and cut holes
in my jeans
with the yellow
little-kid scissors

27

that I still had
in my bedroom.

I ruined
all those clothes
that hugged my body
too tight—
that showed
way too much
of me.

Then I went
and found
my parents
and as casually
as I could
I said,

"I think . . .
I think, maybe—
I think
I might need
some new clothes."

They were confused—
Mom especially—
about those stretches

in my T-shirts
and stains
on my sweatshirts
and holes
in my jeans.

She picked up
one thing after another
and said,
"I didn't
even notice.
How didn't
I notice?"

She took me shopping
that weekend
and I chose
the biggest
baggiest clothes
I could find—
the biggest sizes
the store had
in the kids' section.

"You're sure,"
Mom said,
"this is what you want?"

It was what
I wanted
because it was what
I needed.

So
I told her,

"Yes."

I tried
to hide.

I wore those bigger
baggier clothes
and glued bigger
brighter smiles
on my face.

The worse I felt—

    and I felt
    a little worse
    every day

—the better I pretended
everything was.

But Dave
and Andrew
and Devin—
they weren't
idiots.
And all that fakeness
I was putting out?
It wasn't fun
to be around.

And eventually
my friends and I . . .
we started

to drift.

Bit   by   bit.

That's how
it happens.
At first
you don't
even notice.
But then
one day
you look up
and you realize
that they're all of a sudden
out of reach.

Not that I
was about to do
any reaching.
I didn't
because I understood.
It made sense
that we'd drifted.

It made sense
that those kids—
my former friends—
didn't want
to be around me.

I didn't want
to be around me
either.

It's like this:

For years
your life
is simple.

A straight
straightforward
        line.

But then
one day
things begin
to get messy.

Just

        a little bit.

But then

        a little more

and then

                a little more   still.

And one day
you look up
and realize
the once-straight
line of your life
has doubled back
looped around
tangled itself up
in a knot.

And once that happens
there's no
going back.

You've stepped through
a door
and now the thing
is locked
behind you.

Or no:
it's crazier.

You step through
a door
and then the door
disappears.

Or melts.
Or explodes.
Or
    or
       or
          or turns into
            a chicken
              and runs
                away.

Your life
will never be
as simple
and easy
as it was
again.

Three years.

No—

more.

Three years
and two or three
months.

That's how long ago
Nick said
what he said.

More than three years ago . . .

But I've thought about it—

that handful
of never-ending moments

—every single day
since.

I go
to a school
full of skinny kids
and thin teachers.

Everybody.

Every

body.

I stick out
like a sore thumb.

I stick out
like—

like—

like
a fat kid.

THIN ↗ THINNER ↑ EVEN THINNER ↗ THINNEST ↑

I linger.

I

dawdle.

I take

my

time.

I walk
to school
as slow
as I can
and wait
outside
as long
as I can
hoping
the halls
will clear
so when
I finally
step inside
I won't

44

have to see
a single
person.

So no one
will have
to see

me.

I don't know
who makes the desks
that we have
at my school.

But I know—

I know
for a fact

—that whoever it is
is skinny.

There's no way
a fat person
would make

the space between
the back
of the chair
and the front
of the desk
so narrow.
So narrow
I have to
suck in my stomach
and hunch in my shoulders
and collapse my chest
just to fit
and then sit there
for a 55-minute lecture
on linear functions
feeling squeezed
and pressed
and unable
to forget
for even
a second
how fat
and out of place
and unwelcome
I am.

Mom always offers
to leave me lunch money.

But the thought
of standing there
in the cafeteria
in line
along with everybody—

every
        body

—else
and saying
loud enough
to be heard
over the talking
and shouting
and laughing
and calling
that I
want a sandwich
and chips
and a cookie
and maybe
just in case
for later

another bag
of chips—
it's all
too much.

Too . . .

Too

SOMEthing.

A something
that makes
me squirm
in my sweatshirt
and wish
I didn't
need to eat
at all.

There's a corner
of the cafeteria
no one goes.

All that's there
is a bucket

of gray water
and a dirty mop
and a big bin
with **LOST
AND NOT YET FOUND**
scrawled on the side.

And me.
That's where
I sit.
Me
and the bucket
and the mop
and the bin.
In the corner
no one
goes.

Mostly
I keep my head down.

I take tiny
tiny bites.

I pretend
my lunch
means nothing to me
that I could take it
or leave it
when really
I'm starving
and just want
to get it all
in my mouth
and down to
my stomach
as fast as
I possibly can.

And sometimes—

I can't help it

—sometimes
I look up.

I look
around.

At all
the other kids
talking
and laughing
and eating
like normal
because that's what
they are.

Normal.

Sometimes
I even search
the sea of faces
and find Dave
and Andrew
and Devin—
sometimes
I even look
for Nick Fisher.

I wonder
if he even remembers
that moment

in that hallway
way back
in elementary school.

Probably
not.

For me
it was like
an atom bomb
going off
and wrecking everything
in its path.

But for him
it was probably
just another moment
in another
completely forgettable
day.

And sometimes
when I lift
my head
and look
around—
some days
if I'm feeling brave
I look

    for her.

And it's like—

    I don't know how
    to describe it

—but it's like
I just **KNOW**
where she'll be.
In the lunch line.
At the table
near the bathroom
or the one
by the windows.

Or today—

how I know
to turn my head
toward the doors
just as the things
swing open
and she
comes walking in.

JULES

Jules
is pretty—
sure.

But it's not
her face
that I
always find myself
staring at.
It's what
she's holding
in her hands.

Today
there's a textbook
wrapped up
in a paper bag
and covered
in doodles.
I know this one
and know
if I were closer
I'd see:

a sleepy flower

a sugar-eyed alligator

a happy cloud
raining even happier
kittens.

She's also got
a sketchbook—

the cover closed
and the whole thing
pinched protectively
between a pair
of binders
but a single page
poking out
just enough
for me to see
a smear of pencil
or bit of marker
a hint
of something
larger . . .

Jules draws.
She draws
like me.
And yes—
she's pretty.

She's probably
even beautiful.
But that's not what
keeps me up
some nights—
that's not what
makes my heart race
and my head spin.

No—

it's the flowers
and the alligators
and the clouds
that dump out
all those beautifully drawn
kittens.

I like Jules.

Like . . .

    I **LIKE** like her.

But I'm not
an idiot.

Or not
a big enough idiot
to believe
that a girl like Jules
could like a boy
like me.

She doesn't.

She can't.

She won't.

Not ever.

    Jules can't like me back
    because she
    looks like her

and I
look like me.

Because she
is thin
and I
am **FAT**.

And maybe
it shouldn't be that way.

Maybe
it shouldn't matter
that Jules
looks like her
and I
look like me.

I wish
it didn't matter.

Some days
I wish
so hard
it **HURTS**.

But—

But—

it does matter.

It **DOES**.

I see proof of it
every day.

Thin people
go with thin people.

That's
just how
it works.

Fat people
are never love interests.

Fat people
are never heroes.

If they get
to be anything
at all
fat people
are the stupid sidekicks

the dumb
  clumsy
    ridiculous
    clowns.

When the bell
cries out
across the cafeteria
and everyone gets up
to go
I grab
what's left
of my lunch
and make my way
to the bathroom.
And there
in the safety
of a locked stall
I cram
my sandwich
into my mouth.
I shove
a fistful
of pretzels
past my teeth.
I force

a brownie
down my throat
barely
even pausing
long enough
to chew.

I linger
at the end
of the day.

I stick around
in my classroom
long after
the bell rings
pretending
it takes me forever
to pack my bag
then pretending
I'm fascinated
by a poster
of the periodic table.

I stay
as long as
I can—

leaving only
once Mr. Parker
gathers his stuff
and grabs his keys
getting ready
to leave himself
and lock the door
behind him.

Only then
do I step out
into the hallway
hoping
praying
everyone
has already
made it out
the door
and gotten on to doing
whatever they're doing
with their day.

I don't
head home.

I go

in the opposite
direction—
I go toward
the nearest store.

Because
I'm hungry—

    I'm always
    hungry

—and this morning
before I left
I noticed
that we were out
of the chips
I always eat
after school
and I guess
today
my hunger
is bigger
than my fear
of being out
and about—
of being seen.

I pass
some kids
on my way—
two groups
of four or five each
one older
and one younger.
But luckily
they're both on
the other side
of the street
and don't pay
any attention
to me.

Outside the store
I take a deep breath.
Do I really
want to do this?
Because someone
from school
could be inside.
And even if
the store is empty
of customers
someone has to be
behind the cash register.

And maybe
it's one of those grown-ups
who acts more like a kid
than most kids do.
Maybe
they'll see me
buying chips
and make
one of those comments.

"How about
you grab an apple
instead?"

"You really think
you need more
potato chips?"

"I hope these aren't
all for you."

It's almost enough
to get me turning around
and heading home
chipless.

But my stomach—

my hunger—
it gets me pushing
through the door
and stepping into
the store.

Right away
I check
behind the register.

There
I see
a woman
thumbing away
at the screen
of her cell phone.
She's big.
Even bigger
than me.

Relief
washes over me.
I take another step
into the store
and let the door
swing shut

behind me.

Cold air
hits me
from above.
It cools the sweat
that's pooled beneath
my sweatshirt
and that's lining
the legs
of my jeans.

I don't waste
any time—
I head right for
the chips
reaching for my wallet
and counting the money
inside.
I've got enough
to buy six bags—
and that
happens to be
exactly how many
are on the shelf.
I pile them all up
in the crook of my arm

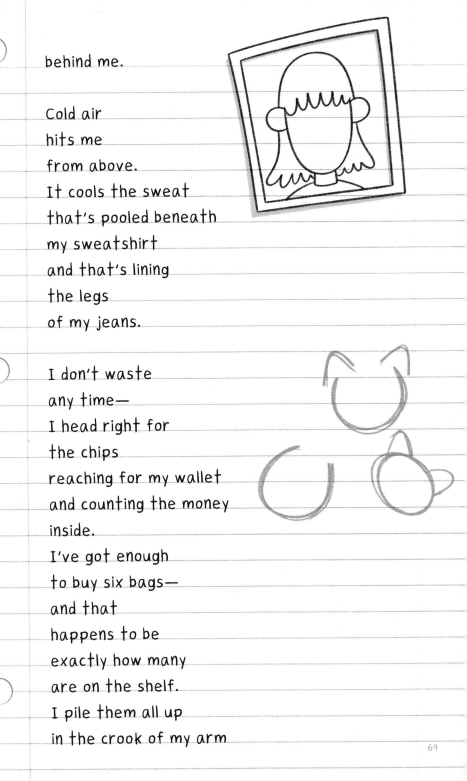

then head back toward
the register.

And I'm halfway down the aisle
when someone else
turns into it.
And the sight of them—
it causes me
to freeze.
Because it's not
just anyone.
It's . . .

        Dave.

Dave.

The kid who
used to come over
every day
after school.

The kid who
used to ask me
to sleep over
every Friday night
and sometimes
Saturday night
too.

The kid who
on multiple occasions
accidentally called my mom
"Mom."

The kid who
I first tried
to stay up
all night with
and finally did
on our fourth try
watching the sunrise

from his back porch
before slogging inside
and sleeping
until noon.

The kid who
loved comics
as much as me
and drew
as much as me
until he decided
he actually wanted
to just be
a writer.

The kid who
made me promise
that we'd both go
to the same college
and be roommates
and that even if
we both got married
we'd still live
in the same house
just so we
could keep hanging out
every single day

and keep making up
our crazy silly
superhero stories.

The kid who
along with Andrew and Devin
came and found me
in the bathroom
after Nick Fisher
blew my world
to bits.

The kid who
called Nick
a jerk
an idiot
a loser
and made a bunch of jokes
about how short he was
and did everything else
he could think to do
to cheer me up
during what was
the worst day
of my life.

The kid who

for years and years
I'd just assumed
would always be
a part—

a big part

—of my life.

Dave.

THAT
Dave.

It's him
coming down the aisle
right toward me.

I almost drop
all those bags
of chips.

But at the last second
I tighten
my grip.

And one bag—
it squeaks
against my fingertips.

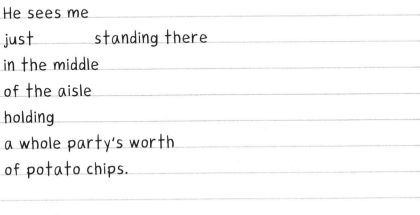

Dave's head
jerks in my direction.

He sees me
just   standing there
in the middle
of the aisle
holding
a whole party's worth
of potato chips.

Crap.

Oh crap
oh crap.

It's cold
in the store—
but sweat sprouts
in my armpits
and on my back
and between
my thighs.

MOVE, will.

Don't just
STAND THERE.

I start
walking.
I walk
toward Dave
and Dave walks
toward me
his eyes
flicking down
gluing themselves
to his shoes.

I shift
my shoulders
hoping

I can rearrange
the folds
of my hoodie
to better hide
my bulges
and lumps
but that—
it just makes
it worse.
Makes it feel
like somehow
the stupid thing
has shrunk.
Like it's pulling
even tighter
across my chest
and breathing—
I can't—
it's hard—
I can't
breathe
and the sweat—
so much
sweat—
my baggy jeans
that aren't baggy
enough—

that can't be baggy
enough—
that are still
too tight
in all the wrong
places
because no one
makes clothes
for a kid
the size and shape
of me—
my stupid
crappy jeans
grate against
my legs
with every step
and rub raw
the insides
of my already-
rubbing-together thighs
so the skin there
turns hot
and wet
and starts
to burn
hotter and
hotter

and hotter
with every
step.

    Ow.

    Ow ow ow.

    Crap.

    Stupid
    stupid
    CRAP.

Here
he is.

Dave.
Dave Capaldo.
David James Capaldo.
My former
friend.
My once-upon-a-time
partner
in crime
who I haven't spoken to
for two

whole years
maybe
even longer.
Dave
wearing a T-shirt
and shorts
that end
above his knees.
His body—

his thin
regular
normal body

—out there
on display
for anyone
everyone
to see.

Dave keeps his eyes
fastened to his shoes
and digs his hands
in his pockets
and as he nears me
as he passes
right by

a few inches
from me
I keep
my head down
and keep
my mouth shut.

I pretend
along with Dave
that the two of us
have never
even met.

I don't dawdle
now.

As soon
as Dave
is out
of sight
I dump
all six
bags of chips
on the nearest shelf
and hurry
down the aisle
and out of
the store
toward home
as fast
as I can
go.
My body—

every single inch
of the whole
entire
thing

—covered

in sweat
soaking
my hoodie
from the inside
out
and my thighs—
the insides of
my thighs—

    rubbing
    rubbing
       and
    grating

—so hot
and raw
and by now
probably bleeding.

Once
I get
inside
I lock
the door
behind me
and for
the first time

in twenty minutes—
the first time
since I spotted Dave
in the store . . .

I take
a breath.

Nice
and slow.

I hold it
in

then let it
out.

And then—

    I don't   want to
    but   I want to
        I   have to

        —I head
         for the kitchen.

I eat.

I eat
and eat
and eat.

Whatever
I can find.

Whatever
I can get
my big
fat hands on.

Pretzels.
Cookies.
Crackers.
Nuts.

And each bite—

    every
    shoveled-in
    mouthful

—overwhelms
my taste buds

and turns down
the noise
in my brain.

Takes me farther
and farther
from that aisle
in that store.

Farther
and farther
from   myself.

Farther
and farther
from   my sad
            crappy
            pathetic
            life.

I eat
and eat
and eat.

More
and more
and more and

more.

And chewing
and swallowing
and chewing
some more
there are moments—

    brief
    beautiful
    blissful
    moments

—when I forget

    who I am

    what I am

    that I am

        at all.

Mom did it again
tonight
at dinner.

Dad was working late
so it was just her
and me
and midway through
my first bowl
of mac and cheese
she goes,

                "Have you thought any more
                about that club thing?"

I haven't.
Of course
I haven't.

But I know better
than to say it.

So
I shrug
and cram some more
mac and cheese
in my face.

Mom reads **ONE** email—

one of the nine thousand messages
my school sends out
each week

—and it's the one
about **CLUBS**.

All this stuff
about how any kid
can start one
and they can be
about anything.

Mom decided
that I should start
a drawing club.

She said she knows
there must be other kids
who like drawing
as much as me.
Sometimes
she even reminds me

about Dave—
how the two of us
used to draw together
all day
every day.
And when I tell her—

AGAIN

—that Dave
stopped caring
about drawing
and making comics
and **ME** —

okay
that last part
I don't say

—years ago
she goes back
to those other kids
that she swears
are out there.
And she swears
too
that if I just start

this stupid club
they'll join it
and we'll all magically become
best friends.

   "Put yourself out there."

That's what she says.
And she said it again
tonight
like nine thousand times.

   "Just put yourself
   out there."

It's maybe
Mom's favorite thing
to say.

That
and also:

   "Just give kids a chance
   to see you.
   To get
   to know you."

But she doesn't
get it.
She's tall
and thin
and has been
all her life.

A kid
who looks
like me . . .

I can't just
        put myself

                    out there.

That's just asking
for trouble.

I think
if I didn't
have to ever again
step foot
in a hallway
school might not
be so bad.

If I could just
hide out
in the back
of classrooms
and draw
my days
away—
maybe
maybe then
I wouldn't dread
getting up
and getting dressed
and coming to this place
over and over
again.

Stupid
stupid
stupid.

You
are so

STUPID.

I was on my way
to second period
and I looked up—

and there she was.

        Jules.

And not Jules
surrounded by friends
like always.

JUST   Jules.

Only   her.

And I knew
how rare
that was.

I knew
it might never happen
again.

And watching her
        come   closer
        and   closer

and   closer
        still
I started
        to wonder . . .

                Maybe.

                        Maybe.

                                What if . . .

                Put yourself
                                out there.

Those words—

        Mom's words

—they were still
banging around
my brain.

        Maybe—

this is what
I was thinking

—maybe
I've been wrong.

Maybe Mom
is right.

Maybe
what if
I just gave Jules—

Jules
who loves drawing
loves doing
the same thing
as me

—what if
I gave her
a chance
to see me?

I kept
my head up.

I looked
right at her—

right at   JULES

—at her eyes
and her mouth
and the sketchbook
she was holding
in her hands.

I looked
and I arranged
my face
into something
that I hoped
looked friendly.

Forty feet.

Another dozen steps
    and she'd be   **RIGHT THERE**.

         We'd be   side by side.

Thirty feet.

     Come on, Will.

     You can do this.

Twenty-five.

     No,
     you **CAN'T**
     do this.

     Will.

     WILL.

     WHAT
     are you
     DOING?

Twenty.

You can do this.

You can do this.

Fifteen.

You idiot.

Ten.

Are you ready?

Of course
you're not ready.

Get ready.

Five.

Open your mouth.

Now is when
you open your mouth
and SAY something.

Do it.

DO IT.

HURRY UP
AND DO—

At the last second
I turned
  away.

Lowered
  my eyes.

Studied
  my shoes.

   I just . . .

   I couldn't do it.

Idiot.

Stupid
stupid
IDIOT.

What's that thing
people say?

When it rains . . .

it **POURS**.

I was sitting there
in study hall.
Just a few hours after
I saw Jules
in the hallway
my brain stuck
on a loop—

stupid
stupid
stupid

—till a sound
shut it up.

"Will Chambers."

Someone
saying it.

A girl.
The one
sitting right
in front of me
in a tank top
army green.

I leaned out
from behind my backpack
which I had up
on my desk
and which I'd been
hiding behind
all period.

A second girl—

> tank top
> white
> with little bits
> of glittery gold
> on the shoulders

—sitting next to the first
said it too.

"Will Chambers?"

My name.

MY name.

> What
> the heck
> is **HAPPENING**?

The second girl—
she said,

"Who's that again?"

I held my breath

and I think I
even winced
like I knew
just KNEW
something bad
was coming
as the first girl
lowered her head
and her voice
and said,

"You know . . .
the fat kid."

As soon as
she said it
the girl's friend—
she got it
she knew
she understood
and then
she giggled
and said,

"The bowl of snot.
I'd definitely take
the bowl of snot."

I wanted to
jam my fingers
in my ears
or maybe
just stab them
with my pencil
so I never
had to hear anything
ever
again.

But
I couldn't.

I couldn't
stop listening.

So I heard
the second girl say,

            "Give me
            another one."

And I heard
her friend say,

            "Okay.

Okay, okay . . .
Would you rather
drink a glass
of someone else's puke—"

"UGH."

"—or kiss
Will Chambers?"

My heart skipped
a beat
then banged out
a crazy
off-kilter
rhythm.
My stomach
made a knot
and squeezed and
squeezed and squeezed
tighter
and tighter
and tighter till
I was pretty sure
it might
just POP
all while

that girl
the second one
said,

"How big a glass?
Or actually—no.
Doesn't matter.
The puke.
I'd take
the puke."

And then
the girls—
they laughed
so loud
so hard
that I'm sure
I could've heard them
even if I **HAD**
stabbed my eardrums
and our teacher—
that's when
he told them
to quiet down
and they did
so I couldn't hear

another word
they said.

But that
didn't matter.
I'd already heard
enough.

I stomped upstairs
as soon as I
got home.
Upstairs
and into
the bathroom.
I slammed
the door
and locked it
even though
no one else
was home.

Then I tore off
my stupid hoodie
and my stupid T-shirt
and my stupid pants
too.

113

And then
I stepped up
to the mirror.

And I looked.

I forced myself

to look.

To look
and look
and look
and look and
look and look
and look.

I looked

at my chubby cheeks

and my double chin

and my flabby arms

and my lumpy chest

and my thick wrists

and my pudgy fingers

and my big belly

and my wide thighs

and my massive legs

and my huge ankles

and my fat feet—

at all of
    fat
      fat
        fat
         fat
          fat
           FAT
            me.

I looked   and felt
   something   bigger
        stronger
        darker
than I'd ever felt
   before.

And the next thing   I knew
I wasn't   just looking
          but
                pushing

                pulling

                pressing

                punching

                ripping

                tearing

                tugging

                hitting

                trying

          trying

        trying

        trying

trying

to   force

my   body

        into

a   smaller
             better
             thinner
                 shape.

I couldn't
do it.

I couldn't push
or press
or punch
or pound
my body
into a smaller
shape.

But I need
to do
SOMEthing.

I don't
want to look
like this
anymore.

I don't
want to be
like **ME**
anymore.

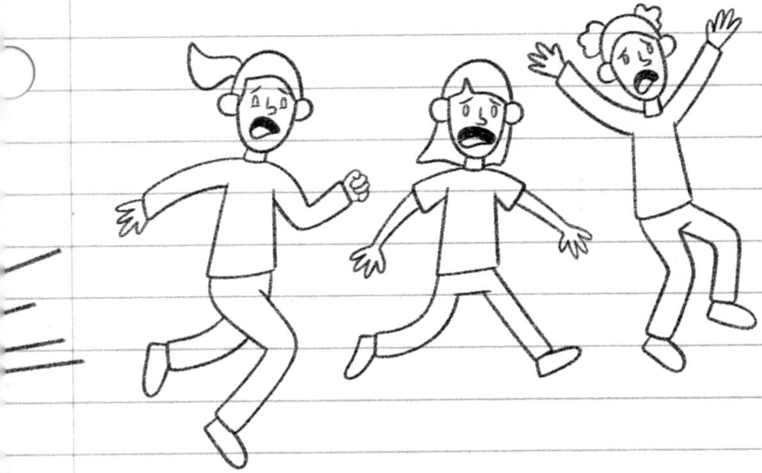

"Will?"

I glanced up
from my notebook
and checked
the clock.

6:07.

My stomach
gave a growl.

I could hear Mom
in the kitchen—
kicking off
her shoes
and putting down
her bags.

"Will!
I've got
a little
surprise
for you. . . ."

That's when
I smelled it.

"I picked up
a pizza
on my way home!"

Next thing I knew
I was on my feet
and heading for
the kitchen
totally ready
to grab that pizza
and devour
every hot
gooey
oily
slice.

But just before
I stepped through
the doorway—
some other voice
sounded out
in my head.
It was my voice
but there was something
about it
that was different—
something

in it
that I'd never
really heard
before.

The voice said,

Wait.

It said,

No.

It said,

Don't.

It said,

How about
we do something
DIFFERENT.

It asked me,

Do you ever see
your skinny mom

or skinnier dad
stuffing their faces
with pizza?

And the answer
was no.

So maybe

maybe
you need to
stop eating
like you have been eating
all your life.

"Will!"

I took
a breath
and stepped
into
the room.

"Hey,"
Mom said
as soon as

she saw me.

"Hot today,
huh?"

I tugged at
my hoodie
pulling the front
away from
my body.

"You hungry?

Want to eat?"

I opened my mouth—
but closed it again
without saying
a thing.

I just stared
at the pizza box
Mom was holding.

I looked—
then forced myself
to turn away.

"Will?
Are you feeling
okay?"

I nodded.

Said,

"I just . . .
I don't
really feel
like pizza."

Mom glanced down
at the pizza box.

"Oh."

I knew
she was confused.

Because I'd never
said no
to a slice of pizza
in my life.

"I'll just . . .

I'll have
what you're having."

Mom frowned.

        "You're gonna eat
        leftover chicken
        and broccoli
        and rice?"

I squirmed
against my sweatshirt.
I shrugged.

But Mom—
she was still
frowning at me.
So I added
a nod.
I added
a bunch of them.
And then
I told her,

        "Yes."

I ate
what Mom ate.

A piece of plain
chicken.

A scoop of brown
rice.

A bunch of steamed
broccoli.

It was
bland.

It was
flavorless.

It was verging on
gross.

Especially
compared
to the pizza
which was still

right there
just sitting out
on the counter.

I wanted it.

I wanted it
so bad.

I wanted
it all.

I wanted every
last slice.

But I couldn't
have it.

You **CAN'T**.

I knew that.

No more pizza.

I know
I know
I know.

Do you want to be
grosser than
a glass of puke
for the rest
of your life?

No.

No
no
no.

No more pizza.

No more pizza
for you.

No more pizza
for big fat stupid ugly
YOU.

I'm still hungry.

I'm still
so hungry.

Stupid chicken.

Stupid broccoli and rice.

———————————————

Go to bed, Will.

Just
go to bed.

Because you're not eating.

You're not eating
another bite
tonight
so you might as well
just go
to bed.

———————————————

No more food.

No more food
    until breakfast.

My stomach
keeps growling
keeps telling me
it's empty
keeps saying
it needs more.
More more more
more more.

But no.

YES.

I ate
what Mom ate.

Exactly
what Mom ate.

And is she
down the hall
sitting up in bed
clenching her teeth
scrawling in a notebook
doing everything she can
to keep herself from charging downstairs
and cramming slices of cold pizza in her face?

No.

Of course
not.

What is wrong
with YOU?

I can't do it.
I **CAN'T**.

Of course
you can't.
Did you really
think **YOU**
could eat chicken
and rice
and broccoli
for dinner?

LOL.

Who
do you think
you are?

He—

WHAT
do you think
you are?

He's—

Normal?

Regular?

Thin?

No.

No no no no no.

I—

You're a **MONSTER.**

Humongous
and always hungry.
Creeping around
and scaring the crap
out of everyone
unfortunate enough
to see you.

A **MONSTER**
always wanting
more.

More more more more
MORE.
So go ahead.

Go and **EAT**.

EAT
like you want to.

EAT
like you know
you want to.

I got out of bed
at 2:15.

I went downstairs
and into the kitchen

DON'T

and opened the fridge

you stupid

and got out the pizza

fat stupid **FAT**

and set the box on the counter

gross dumb

and lifted the lid

disgusting

and pretty much just

ugly idiot

ATTACKED the thing

MONSTER

ate slice after slice

disgusting

taking enormous bites

disgusting

barely chewing before swallowing

disgusting

so I could cram more

you monster

into my mouth

you **MONSTER**

more and more and more and

I hate you

more

I hate you

and more

I HATE YOU

and more

I HATE YOU
I HATE YOU
I HATE YOU.

Never again.

Not ever
again.

I won't
let this happen
again.

This starts
today.

I'm in charge now.

ME.

———————————

No more food
        until lunch.

———————————

I packed my lunch
like always.

But instead of
the towering sandwich
and two or three snacks
and the cookie
or brownie
or both
I only made
the sandwich.

Dad came in
right when I
was finishing up.
He peeked over my shoulder
as he reached for
a coffee cup.

"Is that,"
he asked,
"enough?"

It wasn't.
Not
for me.
But that
is the point.

This
is what
I have
to do.

This
is how
I become
a new me.

A thinner

better

me.

So I said,

"Yep."

I said it
right away
nice and loud
and clear.

And Dad—
he gave my lunch
one last look
then got his coffee
and told me to have
a good day.

First period
was easy.

I still had
all that pizza
from the night before
in my stomach.

But then
during second
that feeling
of being full—
somehow
it just

disappeared.

Suddenly
I was hungry.
So hungry.
Like I hadn't eaten
in weeks.
Like my stomach wasn't
just empty—
but like it had been
scraped clean.

EAT.

No.

FEED ME.

HURRY UP
AND FEED ME.

NO.

YOU KNOW
YOU WANT TO.

I don't.

I don't.

LIAR.

YOU WANT
TO EAT
THAT SANDWICH.

No.

IT'S RIGHT THERE
IN YOUR BAG.

No.

MMMMMM.

IT'S GOT MAYO.

MAYONNAISE.

YOU COULDN'T
STOP YOURSELF
FROM PUTTING
THAT ON
COULD YOU?

YOU LOVE
MAYONNAISE.

No.

YOU LOVE IT
SO MUCH.

I BET
YOU COULD EAT
A WHOLE BATHTUB
FULL OF MAYONNAISE.
JUST SLURP IT UP

WITH A STRAW.
WOULDN'T
THAT
BE NICE?

WOULDN'T THAT
BE FUN?

No.

YES.

NO.

COME ON, WILL.

NO MORE
LYING.

YOU KNOW
IT'S TRUE.

NO.

YOU ARE ME

NO.

AND I AM YOU

NO
NO
NO

AND ABOUT THAT

NO

THERE'S NOTHING

NO!

YOU CAN DO.

Clenching
my teeth
squinching
my eyes
doing everything
I could think
to do
to drown out
that voice
and distract myself
from the signals
my stomach
was sending
my brain
I managed
to make it
through one class
and another
and all the way
to—

NO MORE FOOD UNTIL

—lunch.

I felt
relief.

But then
that got
obliterated
by a kind
of franticness.

I bolted
out of class
like an animal—
like some sort of crazed
creature

SEE?

NO.

YOU SEE?

who just wanted
a safe
quiet corner
to devour
his midday meal.

I was supposed to go
to the cafeteria.
Everyone was.

But I didn't.
I couldn't.
Not today.
I couldn't believe
I HAD been going
all those years.
Looking like I looked.
Feeding myself
in front of all those people.
How
      disgusting.
How
      humiliating.
How
      ugly.
How
      nasty.
How
    GROSS.

I waited
at the edge
of the hallway
and made sure
no one
could see
and slipped out

a side door
and slunk behind
the auditorium
and found a patch
of crusty concrete
surrounded by a bunch
of forgotten
junk.

It felt like
the perfect place
for a monster.

The perfect place
for me.

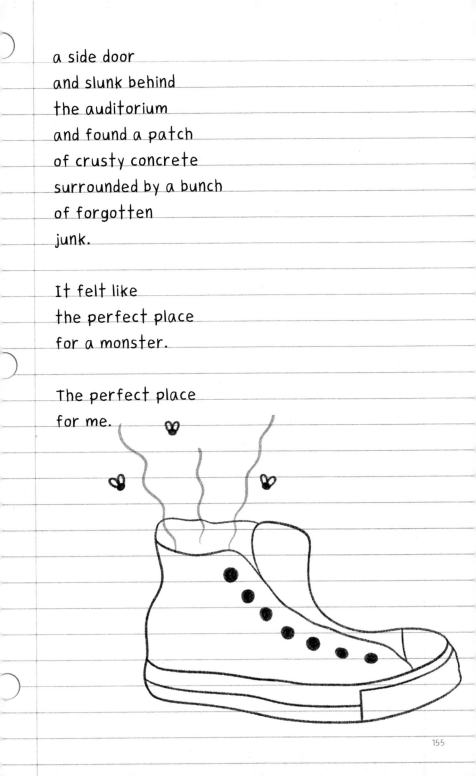

Home.

Home again.

Another afternoon.

Alone.

Alone
and hungry.

But this hunger
is different.

I feel it—
but it feels
smaller
weaker
and I feel
like I know
how it works
how it'll try
to overwhelm me
how it'll try
to control me
how it'll try
to make me

do things
I'm no longer
gonna do.

PROVE IT.

I prove it
by going to the fridge
and pulling out what's left
of the pizza
from the night before.
Two pieces.
I tip the box
and let them slide out
and into the trash.
Right on top of
a little mound of coffee grounds
and a paper towel
soaked in neon-blue
window cleaner.

Then I go
to the cabinet
and gather up
    the cookies
    and crackers
    and donuts

and pretzels
and find
some jelly beans
and peanut butter cups
and little bags
of M&M's
in the drawer—
all the crap
I always ask
my parents
to buy me
every time
they go
to the store—
and I dump
all of that
in the trash
and it makes me
feel good
and strong
and capable
and in control
like I
can really
do this.

Like I

can do
anything
at all.

———————————————

I stopped myself.

Before I threw out
all the food in the house
I made myself
stop
because I couldn't have
my parents
getting suspicious
and asking questions.

Not now.

Not when I was only just
making some progress.

How long
will it take?

How long
till I can look
in the mirror
and see
something different?

How many meals
do I have to skip
before I look
how I want
how I need?

It's easier
today.

And I've figured out
some things
that help
in the moments
it's hard.

If I can get
to a sink
I drink
big gulps
of water—
as cold
as I
can make it.
It numbs
my tongue
and fools
my stomach
into thinking
it's been fed.

And if I can't

get up
and go
to the bathroom
for a second
or third time
during class
I bite
my lip—
dig my teeth
into the skin
and focus
on that pain
instead of
the growling
in my belly.

And if I still
can't stop thinking
about eating—
about sneaking
a bite
of the sandwich
I let myself bring
for lunch
or going down
to the cafeteria
and ramming my fist

through the glass
of the vending machine
and gobbling down
every last bag of chips
and package of cookies
inside—
if I can't
shut up
the voice
telling me

EAT

I remind myself
how bad
I want this.
How much
I need this.
How this
is the way
I change
my life.

This
is the way
I fix
everything.

This
is the way
I fix
me.

Chicken
and broccoli
and rice
for dinner.

"You really want
the same thing?"
Mom asked
while making
a new batch.

"Yeah,"
I told her.
"I actually—
I really like it."

She doesn't
believe me.

Or she does—

but I can see
in her eyes
that she knows
something weird
is going on.

"What?"
I say
forcing
a smile.
Even giving her
a breathy
little laugh.
And then
I say
this thing
she always says.
I say,
"Your baby
is growing up."

And hearing that
she can't help
but smile back.
"Well . . . ,"
she says
lifting the lid

on the rice pot
and giving it
a stir
"Okay."

Why didn't I do this
sooner?

I should've done this
sooner.

Today
out back
behind the auditorium
I didn't even need
my whole sandwich.

I ate half.

Then one more
bite.

And then I threw
the rest of it
in the trash
on my way
to history class.

It's a good
morning.

A very
very good
morning.

My jeans—
I woke up
and put them on
and they felt

different.

They weren't
biting into
my body
like usual.

And when I tried
I could fit
a whole finger
and the tip
of another
between my hip

and the waistband.

They're **LOOSE.**

    At least
    a little bit.

And I know
that sometimes
jeans get loose
on their own
and that once
you wash them
they go back
to being tighter.
But I really
don't think
this is that.
I really think
it's happening.
I think
I'm really
just a little bit

      thinner.

I dug through my closet

and found
a belt.

Mom bought it for me
a couple years ago
when we had to go
to her friend's wedding.
I wore it then
but never again.
Because I never
needed it.
And I don't
really need it
now.
But I will
soon.

Soon
I'm gonna need
a whole new
wardrobe.

No more food
   until dinner.

Soon
I'll be good enough.

Soon
I'll be thin enough.

Soon
I'll be able
to stop hiding
at home
and in hoodies
and behind
the auditorium
and at the back
of classrooms.

Soon
I'll be thin enough
to do
what Mom's
always telling me
to do—
put myself

out there.

Give kids

a chance
to look
and see
me.

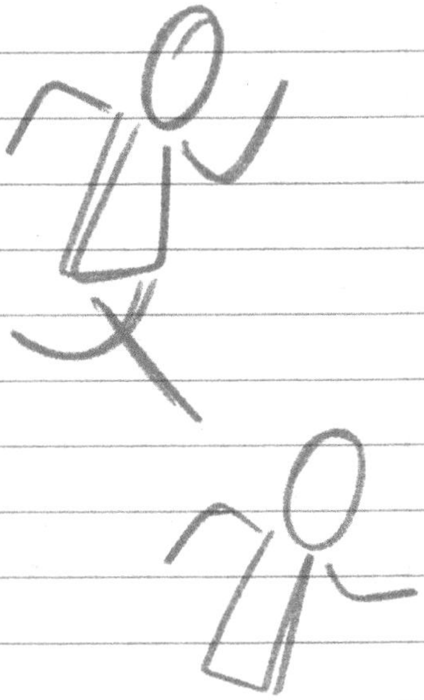

I was out back
behind the auditorium
alone
unseen
when all of a sudden

Crck-crck FWOOH

Crck-crck FWOOH

Crck-crck FWOOH.

It took me
a second
but then
I realized—
a skateboard.
It was the sound
of a skateboard
racing over
the squares
of a sidewalk.

Next thing

I knew
this kid—

    long black
    hair
    tight black
    jeans
    fluorescent-pink
    fingernails

—he came tearing
around
the corner
and out onto
my patch
of crusty
concrete.

    SKRRRT.

That was the sound
of his sneaker
pressing down
on the pavement
and skittering him
to a stop.
He looked

at me.
I looked
at him.

I'd never seen him
before.

Never seen anyone
like him
either.

I was too
surprised
to be nervous.

"Hey,"
he said.
"I was just—"

He hooked a thumb
over his shoulder
toward where
he'd come from.

"There's this woman.
She keeps yelling at me
for not being in the cafeteria."

"Mrs. Antolini,"
I said
not even realizing
I'd opened
my mouth.

The kid smiled
when he heard my voice.

"The attendance monitor,"
I explained.

"And you **HAVE** to be
in the cafeteria
during lunch?"
the kid asked me.

I nodded.

"Brutal,"
he said.
"Cafeterias
are the **WORST**."

I agreed.
But I didn't know
what to say

or do
to let him
know it.
I didn't know
if I should say
or do
anything
at all.

How long
had it been
since I'd said
more than four words
to another kid?

   "So."
   He rolled his board
   back and forth
   so the wheels clacked
   on the concrete.
   "You mind?
   Will it bother you
   if I skate
   back here?"

I shrugged
because I thought

in the moment
that shrugging
was a cool
laid-back thing
to do.

But then I worried
that the kid might think
a shrug meant
I wasn't sure
about him being there
and the truth was
that I wanted him
to stay.
The truth—
as weird
and sudden
as it was
—was that I wanted him
to stay—

I really
really wanted him
to stay

—so that I
could go on looking

at him.

And it wasn't
because of his clothes
or his hair
or his fingernails.
What it was—

what I think
it was

—was the way
he looked at me
and talked to me
so plainly
so normally
like he didn't find it
the least bit weird
that I was back there
behind the auditorium
all by myself
when I was supposed to be
in the cafeteria
with everybody else.

So I quickly added,
"No."

I said,
"Not at all."

I said,
"Go for it."

And he
told me,
"I appreciate it."

Then he hopped on
his board
and began
to skate.

I drew
in my notebook
and pretended not
to watch the kid
though all
I was doing
was watching
the kid.

He was good
at skateboarding.
Really good.

Not that I know
the first thing
about what makes someone good
at skateboarding.

But it was obvious
just watching him
soaring up
and hanging there
high in the air
all while his board
did these crazy spins
beneath him
only to then

sink back down
his feet right where
they were supposed to be
so he'd land
so cleanly
and then so smoothly
just keep rolling
right along.

I watched his feet
and his arms
and his legs—
but mostly
I watched his face.

He looked

     so relaxed.

So

    CONFIDENT.

That's what
it was.

That's what

I couldn't believe.

What I couldn't
get enough of.

The way he was
so sure
that he could make
his body
do exactly what
he wanted it
to do.

Eventually
he hopped off his board
and dug a wad of foil
out of his backpack.
He unwrapped it
and inside
was a bagel
loaded up
with cream cheese.

"You already eat?"
he asked me
taking a big bite
of his lunch.

"Wha . . . ?"

I wasn't
expecting
a question.
And definitely not
THAT question.

"I, ah—
yeah.
I . . .
yeah."

The kid
kept looking
at me.
But I
dropped my eyes
and crunched in
my shoulders
curling my body
into my notebook
and making myself
as small
as I could.

The bell rang—
and a part of me
was glad
for an excuse
to get up
and leave.

But another part of me—
it had been hoping
ever since
the kid showed up
that the bell
wouldn't ring
at all.

"Thanks again,"
he said.

Then:
"I'm Markus,
by the way."

"Will,"
I told him.

And just before
he pushed off

the pavement
and rolled
away
he added,
"I guess
I'll see you
around."

And now . . .

Now I can't
stop thinking
about him.

Markus.

"I guess
I'll see you
around."

Did he mean it?

Did he mean
he planned
to come back?

Do I even
want him to?

I don't know.

I don't
know.

All I know
is that I can't stop thinking
about it.

Thursday

I'm up.

Awake
without even needing
my alarm.

And I'm . . .

Nervous?

Excited?

I don't
know.

All I know
is that for the first time
in a long time
I actually want
to go to school.

I have
a glass of water
for breakfast.

Then I tuck my lip
between my teeth
bite down hard
and head
to school.

Is he gonna
come back?

What do I do
if he
comes back?

I guess
I was hurrying
and got out back
earlier
than usual.

I took out my notebook
just like always
but didn't actually
draw.

I was too busy

waiting
and listening.
Listening
and waiting.

A couple minutes
passed.

Then a couple
more.

More time
than anyone would need
to get out back
behind the auditorium
even if they weren't
on a skateboard.
Even if they stopped
in the bathroom
first.
Even if
their third-period class
ran a little late.

He's not coming.

OF COURSE

he's not coming.

Why would he
come?

Why would **HE**
want to look at
or talk to
YOU?

My stomach roared.

EAT.

I squeezed
my eyes shut.
Bit
my lip.

You're such
an idiot.

Did you really think—

Crck-crck FWOOH

Crck-crck FWOOH.

My eyes
flew open
and I saw him
Markus
swerving around
the corner.
Same black jeans
and tight T-shirt
though today
his hair
was piled up
and rubber-banded
atop his head
and his fingernails
were painted yellow
instead of pink.

      "Busted again,"
      he said.
      "By Mrs. What's-Her-Face—
      Antelope Panini?"

     "Antolini,"
     I said—
     heart pounding
     lungs aching
     lips turning up

into a grin.

"Close enough."
Markus smiled.

"You cool
with me
being back here
again?"

"Cool,"
I said.
"Yes.
Definitely—
yes."

Markus skated
for fifteen minutes
then got off his board
and dug in his backpack
for his lunch.
He sat on his board
and rolled back and forth
as he took bites
and chewed
and swallowed.

He wasn't looking
at me.
He was just

    staring off.

But I could tell—

    at least
    I was pretty sure—

he was gonna look over
any second
and speak.

My heart

was pounding
all over again.

   You can
   do this.

   How do
   I do this?

      "So,"
      Markus finally
      said.
      "What's
      your deal?
      Why aren't you
      in the cafeteria
      either?
      What's
      your story?"

I don't know what
I'd been expecting.
Maybe a question
about if I had
any brothers or sisters
or if I had
any pets.

Wasn't **THAT**
the sort of thing
you were supposed to ask someone
you just met?

"My . . .
story?"

Markus nodded.

And then he looked down
at my notebook
which I had open
in my lap.

"You're an artist,"
he said
squinting
and tipping his head
so he could see
what I'd been working on.

But I—
I slammed it shut
before he could see
much of anything.

And Markus's eyes
bounced back up
and got narrow
and I can't—
it's hard
to explain—
but it's like
I'd slammed my notebook
to keep him from seeing
too much
of **ME**
but by slamming my notebook
I'd actually shown him
ALL
of me.

And then—

No no no.

DON'T.

Don't mess
this up.

—I freaked.

"What's **YOUR**
story?"
I spat.
"Why are **YOU**
back here?"

Markus
leaned back.
He looked . . .
surprised.
But only
for a second.
Then
he did
the weirdest
thing.

He just

       answered.

———————————

"I move a lot. It's because of my dad. His
job. They send him to all these different
sites. We're usually only in a place for a
few months. Once—one time, we stayed in
this town for a little over a year. Fourteen

months, I think? That's the record. That's the longest we've ever been in the same place. I guess the site my dad was working on was really messed up. I don't know. But different towns, different cities—it means different schools, obviously. So, let's see . . . I think this is my seventh? Or eighth. Yeah. My eighth middle school. Though there was one I didn't even get to go to. Two summers ago, we moved in July, and I was gonna go to the school in that town, but then we ended up moving again in August, so I never got to go. But anyway. At all those different schools—I used to always try to, you know, fit in. Everywhere I went. I used to really make an effort. And I guess my parents feel guilty about moving me around so much, even though it's what we've always done, so every time we get to a new place, my mom takes me out shopping. She buys me stuff. Not cause I ask or anything. But it makes her feel better about moving me, I guess. And what I used to do—I used to wait a few days, until I'd figured out what the kids at whatever new school I was at were all about. THEN I'd have Mom take me out. And I'd get all the right clothes. The right . . . THINGS. You know. The same kind of backpack all the popular kids had. The same headphones or whatever. And I was good at it. I was really, really good at fitting in. Or sort of like changing myself to MAKE myself fit in. And so I knew, even though everything around me was always changing, even though I could never get too comfortable in any place, since I knew we could be moving again at any moment—even though all that, I knew, wherever I went, I could slip in with a group of friends, be liked, get invited to sit with kids at lunch and go to their houses after school and all that. And for a little while, for the first few times—all that made me . . . HAPPY isn't the right word. Or maybe it is. But it wasn't a legit sort of happy. You know? It felt—it felt kinda fake. And it just got so . . . exhausting. And it got more and more uncomfortable, too. Every time. And then one time, when Mom took me out for our usual shopping trip, I just . . . I don't know. I sorta said, Screw it. I decided I'm just gonna wear and do and BE exactly who and what I want to be. ME. Right NOW. And even though that might change—even though what's ME is probably gonna change a whole bunch over time—at least it's still always ME. You know? No matter what's going on around

me, no matter where I am—that's always
gonna be true. And the more I thought about
that, the more I just kept checking in with
myself, kept trying every day to be as ME as
I could possibly be—the more I did that, the
more I couldn't NOT do it. The more I did it,
the harder it was to be anybody BUT me. The
harder it was to act, even for a second, like
some other, not-true version of me. Even if
I didn't fit in super well. Even if I didn't fit in
at all. And don't get me wrong. I'm not saying
I'm the greatest person in the world or
anything. I'm a work—"

The bell rang.

It rang
right in the middle
of Markus telling me
his story—
right in the middle
of me
staring at him
dumbfounded
as he talked
and talked

and talked
sharing
so much
about himself.

The bell rang—
but Markus
didn't get up
to go.
He didn't
start talking again
either.
He just
sat there
and stared back
at me.
And I got
the sense
that he would've
gone on sitting there
and talking
until he finished.
Or even longer.
For the rest
of the afternoon.
Maybe even
all night.

He left it up
to me.

He'd opened
a door
and he was letting me decide
if I wanted
to walk through it.

And I wanted
to sit there
and listen—
and I wanted
to get up
and run.
Because I had the feeling
that once I stepped through
that door
I couldn't
go back
and that once
Markus was done
telling HIS story
it'd be my turn
to talk
and talk
and talk

and share
so much—

TOO much.

And that second want—
that's what
won out.

I got up.
Shoved my notebook
in my bag.
Gave Markus
an awkward nod
and left.

But what if
I'd stayed?

What if
I'd stayed
and listened?

What if
I'd stayed
and told him
my story?

What **IS**
my story?

FAT FAT
FAT FAT
FAT FAT
FAT

FAT FAT FAT FAT FAT
FAT FAT FAT FAT

FAT
FAT FAT
FAT FAT FAT FAT FAT FAT
FAT
FAT
FAT FAT FAT
FAT
FAT FAT FAT
FAT FAT
FAT FAT FAT

Tomorrow.

If he comes back
again
tomorrow
I'll do it.

If he gives me
a sign
that he really
truly
wants
to know—
I'll tell him.

I'll tell him
about Nick Fisher
and Dave and Andrew and Devin
and Jules
and my parents
and maybe
about eating
how I do it
how I've always done it
and how I'm not
anymore
except dinner

so Mom and Dad
don't get
suspicious.

Maybe.

Maybe
I'll put myself

out there.

Maybe
I'll step through
that door
and tell him
every
thing.

I feel like
I'm on
a roller coaster.

Not in the middle
of the ride
but at the very
beginning.

Slowly
slowly
slowly
climbing up
and up and
up
that first
big hill.

And it's like
I'm stuck
in that moment
at the top—
that second

that st r e t c h e s

  out
that goes on
and on and
on
so you feel
more fear
and excitement
and energy—

     so you feel
     more ALIVE

—in that second
than you've felt
all your life.

I'm just   hanging
                    here

                    feeling.

                    Feeling
                and waiting

                     for the ride
                      to begin.

Is this
what it feels like
to make
a friend?

I don't
remember.

I don't
remember
if this is what
it was like
with Dave
or Andrew
or Devin.

But
I think . . .

Is Markus
trying to be
my friend?

Maybe
maybe
maybe.

What if?

As I step
through the doors
and into school
I'm not thinking—

for the first time
in a long time

—about the fact
that I'm entering
a hallway
crammed with kids.
Kids
who will look at me
and think
and whisper
or even
just say
out loud
all the things
they always
do.

No—
I'm only thinking
about Markus
and our spot

out back
and how in just
a few hours
I'll be out there
with him.

I'm not thinking
about anything
else.
I'm definitely
not thinking
about Jules.

Not until
I spot her
up ahead—
up ahead
and heading
right toward me.

And then
I can't think
about anything
else.

She's with
a friend.

Arm
in arm.

Heads tipped
and touching
like they're telling
secrets.

Run.

Get out of here.

She can't see you.

Not yet.

I peer
around
but there's nowhere
to run
to.

No
bathroom.

No
classroom.

I'm
trapped.

No no no no no.

DO something.

She can't
see you yet.

You haven't changed
enough.

You're not good
enough.

You're not thin
enough.

I'm about
to turn around
and hurry back
the way I came—
maybe

back outside
to wait
until Jules
has gotten
to class—
but then
I see
that it's
too late—
I waited
too long—
and here
she is—

    Jules
    and her friend

—stopping
in front of me—

    directly
    in front of me

—because I'm standing
in the middle
of the hallway—
because I'm blocking

their way
with my fat
terrible body.

I should have
run.

You should run
right **NOW.**

But I
can't—
I can't
get my body
to do
what I want
it to do.

I can only
stand there
and stare
like a deer
like an exceptionally stupid
deer
caught in a pair
of extraordinarily bright
headlights.

And I watch
Jules's eyes—

    Jules's bright
    brown eyes

—bounce down
to my feet
and then up again
taking me in—

    my body

—in one
quick
go.

RUNRUNRUNRUNRUN
YOU FAT DISGUSTING—

Laughter bursts
from Jules's friend's lips.

A great
big
GUSH
of it.

Then Jules—
she's grimacing
like she's in pain
like I've somehow
HURT her
and she lowers
her head
and tugs
at her friend
and steers
herself
around me.

I'm not sure
how long
I stood there.

A deer.

A stupid deer.

Eyes glazed.
Empty.

Feeling—

        even though the car
        veered away
        at the very last
        second

—like I'd been hit
run over
left for dead
on the side
of the highway
in the middle
of that hallway.

I'm not sure

how long
I stood there
or how long
I would've gone on
standing there
if the bell
hadn't rung
and gotten me
moving.

But
the bell
        rang.

And then

                        I fled.

I went
to the nearest
bathroom.

To the nearest
mirror.

I gripped
the edges
of the sink
and leaned in
to the glass
and glared
into my stupid
FAT
wild
eyes.

You haven't done
enough.

You'll never do
enough.

You'll never be
enough.

Not ever
ever
ever.

STUPID
STUPID

STUPID

FAT

UGLY
STUPID

IDIOT

It was lunchtime
and I wasn't thinking.

I just went
out back
behind the auditorium.

And two minutes
after I sat down
I heard it.

Crck-crck FWOOH

Markus
coming for me.

"Hey."

I don't
look up.

I focus
on my notebook.

I scribble
and scrawl
turn the page
into a big
black knot.

"Oh-kay . . ."

Markus skates.

And I scribble
and scrawl
and scrape.

Ten minutes
pass.

Maybe
twenty.

And every
minute—

     every
     SECOND

—I'm more angry
and hungry
and mad
and hungry
and angry
and hungry
and—

       "Listen."

Scribble.
Scrawl.
Scrape
scrape
scrape.

     "I'm gonna
     say something.
     I need to ask . . ."

Scrapescrapescrape

scrapescrape.

"Aren't you
ever hungry?"

My hand
my whole arm
my whole entire
body—
it all
seizes up.

"It's just . . .
I never
see you eating
and it's lunch
and I know
we're not allowed
to eat
in class."

I can't—
can't move.

"I only ask
because I know—"

"NO,"
I hear
another voice
growl.

Me.
Mine.
MY voice.

And now I'm looking
right at Markus.
Glaring
at his long
skinny arms
and longer
skinny legs
and his flat
stomach
and narrow
face.
I'm on
my feet.
I'm
angry.
Hungry.
Hurting.
Hating.

"You **DON'T**
know.
You don't
know anything
about me."

He nods.
And lifts
his hands
like he's trying
to get me
to chill.

"Okay,"
he says.
"You're right.
But can you—
can we—
could we
just talk?"

"**NO**."

"Will,
I just—"

"**NO**."

He lowers
his hands.
Lets them drop
to his sides.

And before
he can say
another word
I grab
my bag
and bolt.

Back
in the bathroom.

A different one
this time.

The first one
I'd been able
to find.

I barreled inside
and headed straight
for the stall.
Staggered in
locked the door
and took a seat
on the toilet.

My heart—
it's beating
so fast
too fast
my blood
roaring
in my ears.

Deep breath.

I—
I can't.

My lungs—
they don't—
they won't—
I can't
get them to—

The door
swings open
and more kids
come in.

Two more.

Two

GIRLS.

Talking fast.
In the middle of
a conversation.

What?

What the—

What's
going on?

Why—
what—
why are they
here?

Or—
did I?

Oh no.

I did.

I—
I wasn't
looking
wasn't
thinking
and I went—
I went into
the wrong
bathroom.

IDIOT.

I pick
my feet up.
Lift them
as quickly
and quietly
as I can.

I hold
my breath
and wait
and listen
and hope
and pray
and—

"I knew it.
I **KNEW**
she liked
someone."

"Yeah.
But **WHO**?
Why won't she just
TELL us?"

"I know,
I know.

But she's always
been weird
about these things.
That's just
her.
That's just
Jules."

That
name—
her
name—
I heard it
and felt it
like a knife
        digging
and twisting
and—

"I guess.
But—UGH.
I just want
to KNOW."

"I think
it's Aiden."

"Aiden?
Really?
I was gonna say
Jayden."

"Aiden,
Jayden—
maybe it's
BRAYDEN."

Laughing.

Laughing laughing
laughing

as I picture
those kids
in my head
all of them
thin
thinner
than thin
as thin
as
can
be.
Because thin people

go with thin people
not—

"Or maybe—"

Laughing.

"What?
Who were you
gonna say?"

"I was gonna—
maybe
it's that kid.
Will."

The
bathroom—
the whole
entire
world
teeters
and tips
and I—
I have to brace myself
to keep
from falling.

"Is it
Chalmers?
Will Chalmers?
Chalkers?
Chambers?"

"Chambers!"

LAUGHING LAUGHING LAUGHING.

"Oh my gosh.
Can you
imagine?"

"He's such
a creep.
Always staring
at her
in the hallway."

"Yuck."

Laughing

laughing.

"Anyway.
We'll get it
out of her.
Tonight.
At the sleepover."

"Whoa,
I forgot—
it's Friday.
Okay.
YES.
Tonight.
For **SURE**."

The sink
running.

The dryer
blowing.

The door
opening.

The girls
going.

Gone.

I lower
my feet
and try
to breathe
and bite
my lip
and feel
it bleed
and taste
the blood
and grab
my face
and dig
my fingers
in my eyes
and make it hurt
and hurt
so loud
it fills
my head
until
there's nothing
nothing else
but it.

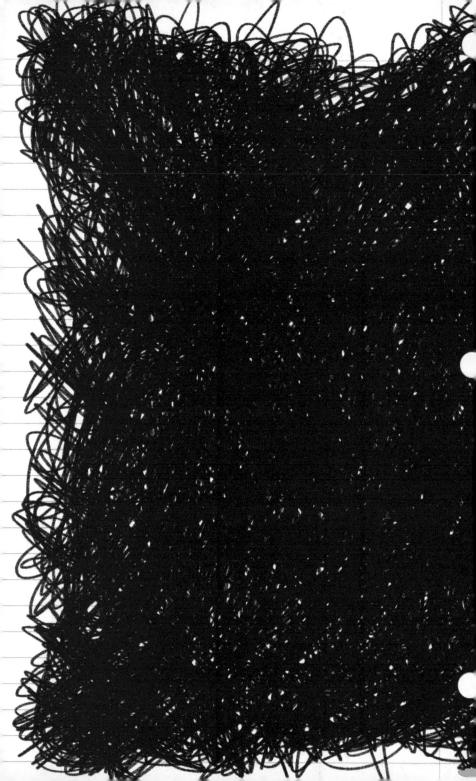

You'll never
be good enough.

No more food.

You don't
deserve it.

I will not eat.

I will not eat.

I will
not eat.

"Will?"

Mom.

"Will!
I made
dinner!"

"I'm not

hungry!

I ate

a big

lunch!"

Hungry.

So   hungry.

                    So

hungry
hungry
hungry

hungry.

        Don't.

        Don't

        do it.

        You can't

        do it.

        You can't
        eat.

"Hey, bud."

Dad. In
the morning.

"You eat yet?
I was gonna
make pancakes."

                    "Yeah.

          I   ate.

          I'm

                              good."

Hungry.

Hungry
   hungry
        HUNGRY.

   Don't.

   Don't.

                              EAT.

                         You need
                         to **EAT.**

   I won't.

            I
   won't.

                              EAT.

   I will not   **EAT.**

   I WILL
        NOT
              EAT.

I WILL
NOT   EAT.

I WILL
NOT EAT.

I WILL NOT EAT

I WILL NOT EAT

I WILL NOT EAT
I WILL NOT EAT
I WILL NOT EAT
I—

"Will?"

Mom.

"Dinner!"

"I'm doing

homework!

I've got

homework!

I've

got

this   project!"

No
no
no
no
no
no

No
no
No

No

no

no

no

No

NO

NO

NO

NO

NO

NO

NO

NO

I WILL NOT EAT

I WILL NOT EAT

I WILL NOT EAT
I WILL NOT EAT

I WILL NOT EAT

I WILL NOT EAT
I WILL NOT EAT
I WILL NOT EAT
I WILL NOT EAT
I WILL NOT EAT

I WILL NOT EAT
I WILL NOT EAT
I WILL NOT EAT

I WILL NOT EAT
I WILL NOT EAT
I WILL NOT EAT
I WILL NOT EAT
I WILL NOT EAT
I WILL NOT EAT
I WILL NOT EAT
I WILL NOT EAT

259

I WILL NOT EAT I WILL NOT EAT
I WILL NOT EAT I WILL NOT EAT I
WILL NOT EAT I WILL NOT EAT I
WILL NOT EAT I WILL NOT EAT
I WILL NOT EAT I WILL NOT EAT
I WILL NOT EAT I WILL NOT
EAT I WILL NOT EAT I WILL NOT EAT I
WILL NOT EAT I WILL NOT EAT I
WILL NOT EAT I WILL NOT EAT
I WILL NOT EAT I WILL NOT EAT
I WILL NOT EAT I WILL NOT EAT I WILL
NOT EAT I WILL NOT EAT I WILL NOT
EAT I WILL NOT EAT I WILL NOT EAT
I WILL NOT EAT I WILL NOT EAT
I WILL NOT EAT I WILL NOT EAT I
WILL NOT EAT I WILL NOT EAT I
WILL NOT EAT I WILL NOT EAT
I WILL NOT EAT I WILL NOT EAT I WILL
NOT EAT I WILL NOT EAT I WILL NOT
EAT I WILL NOT EAT I WILL NOT EAT
I WILL NOT EAT I WILL NOT EAT I WILL
NOT EAT I WILL NOT EAT I WILL NOT
EAT I WILL NOT EAT I WILL NOT EAT I
WILL NOT EAT I WILL NOT EAT I WILL
NOT EAT I WILL NOT EAT I WILL
NOT EAT I WILL NOT EAT I WILL NOT
EAT I WILL NOT EAT I WILL NOT EAT
I WILL NOT EAT I WILL NOT EAT I WILL
NOT EAT I WILL NOT EAT I WILL NOT EAT

morning

monday

morning

i wake   up

                slow

not

                sure

        am i

still

                        asleep?

somehow

        some   how

out of bed

out of

the house

some   how

all   the way

to

school

all   the way

to   the hall

the hall   way

the long

looo o o o o o o o o n   g

hallway

on

my way

to   english

i think

or   math

or

english

down
down

down

just   floating

down

light as   anything

light

                            as

                                        air

down

down

d

o

w

n

                un   til

       it all

every   thing

       teeters

        t

         i

          p

         s

and

i guess

i

trip

and

THWAMP

Ow

OW

ow ow ow ow OW OW OW

"Are you

all   right

dude?"

"Yeah

you   hit

265

                              that   locker

                              pretty hard."

          ow ow ow ow

     down
     down

     float   ing

     down

     am i

                              asleep

     i am

                              asleep
     i   should

          go back   to   sleep

               "Will.

Will?"

i know

that voice

"WILL."

no

you don't

you don't
know me

you don't
know any   thing
about

me

"WILL.

What's—

Are you—
Let me

take you
to   the nurse.

You—"

you don't
know any   thing

"—need to see
the—"

i   yell.

i   think.

i try
to yell
but noth   ing

but he
him
mar   kus

does   n't go
a   way

so i

UGH.

i   shove

    i try   to

shove   him

                    out of

                        my

                            way

    but   every

                    thing

                teet   ers

                                    t

                                    i

                                    p

                                    s

    and   i

        i

            am fall   ing

269

  down

                                        down

                                        down

                                            down

              FWOOMP

                          thunder

              fills   my head
      and

              OW
              OW
              OW
              OW
              OH MY
              OWOWOWOW

                    it's too   bright

                          to see

WILL!

WILL?

SOMEONE GET

SOMEONE GO

CALL THE

the bright

burns   brighter

and then

fades

till all   i see

is

black

Will

what

did he

how

it's gonna be

you're

a ceiling

my ceiling

my bedroom   ceiling

because I'm here

because I'm in   my bed

"Easy.
Easy,
sweetie."

Mom.

My mouth
is sandy
but sweet.

Graham crackers
I think.

"Easy.
Easy.
Nice
and slow."

I finish
sitting up.

"Hi, Mom."

She   laughs
           sniffles
           smiles
           cries.

"Why
are you
crying?"

"I just . . ."

She drags a hand
over her nose
then reaches for
a glass of water.

"Here."

She holds the glass
to my lips
then uses
her other hand
to tip
my head back.

I drink.

And the water—
the regular old
lukewarm water—
tastes incredible.

It makes
me feel   alive.

But
        also

                tired.

So

                tired.

I lie
back
down.

            "Easy.
            Easy,
            honey."

        "Hi, ceiling."

            Mom laughs
                cries

                and

                            and I . . .

There's a bump
on the back
of my head
the size
of an egg
and I'm tired
so
tired
even though
I've spent
the past day
pretty much
doing nothing
but sleeping.

Time for
another
nap.

When I woke up—

when I finally
woke up
fully
for good

—my head
was so clear.

It's like—

I don't know
if this makes
any sense

—it's like
my head
was **RINGING**.

And the light—

the sun
coming through
the window

—it looked

impossible.
Unreal.
Like daylight
manufactured
for a movie.

I looked
around my room.
Saw the crack
in the wall
up in the corner
right below
the ceiling.
Saw the book
upside down
on the shelf
that I always meant
to flip.
Saw George—
my pink elephant.
My favorite stuffed animal
from when I was
a little kid
that I hadn't touched
in years
but couldn't bring myself
to get rid of.

Suddenly
I got the urge
to get up
and fix that book
and grab George
and feel his fur
between my fingers
but when I tried
to sit up—

UGH.

I couldn't
move.
My body
was like one
big bruise.

I lay
back down
and closed
my eyes
and that's when
things began
coming back to me.

Slowly.

And then—

all at once.

Teetering down
the hallway.
Tipping into
a locker.
Shoving Markus
then falling over
myself.
And before that
the days
weeks
of eating less
and less
and then nothing
at all.

And the second
all of it
was back
in my head
I leaped
out of bed.

My body

cried out
with aches
and pains.
It told me
to lie
back down.

But
I couldn't.

I was scared.

Scared
to be alone.

Scared
of myself.

Scared
of what I'd done
to myself.

Scared
of what I could've done
to myself.

So I kept

walking.
Making noise
in the hallway.
Stomping.
Marching.
Wanting
to hear
the sound
of **BEING** there.

Of being

   alive.

I found Mom
and Dad
downstairs
sitting at
the kitchen table
with coffee cups
and napkins
and newspapers
like they'd been sitting there
waiting for me
for weeks.

They stood up

both of them
scraping their chairs back
as soon as I stepped
into the room.

Mom hurried over
and hugged me
tight.
Squeezed
and squeezed
grinding
her teeth
with the effort
like she couldn't
possibly
squeeze hard
enough.

Dad joined
a moment later.
He set his hand
on my back
and kissed the side
of my head.
Just held
his lips there
against

my hair
and didn't
pull away.
I could hear
and feel
the breath
coming in
and out
of his nose
and the stubble
on his chin
scratching
the side
of my face.

And I . . .

    I cried.

I cried
like I hadn't cried
since I
was four
years old.
I cried
with my entire
body.

Jerking.
Rocking.
Sobbing.
Pouring
tears.
Leaking
snot.

Mom
held me.

So did
Dad.

And minutes
passed.

A lot
of them.

But my parents
didn't budge.

They didn't
let go.

They stayed

right where
they were
while I cried
and cried
and cried.

I sat down
at the kitchen table
and Mom sat
next to me
and Dad got me
a glass of water
then sat down
too.

I kept
taking sips.
Small ones.
Dragging each one
out.
Delaying.
Not knowing
what to say
but knowing
I had to say
something.

"I . . ."

Sip.

Sip
sip.

My glass
was empty
and now
I had to pee
and Dad
was getting up
to get me more.

I grabbed the glass
before he could take it
and I tried
again.

"I . . ."

But where
was I
supposed
to start?

"I really . . .

I don't . . .

I really
don't like
being me."

───────────────

I told them
as much as
I could.

It was hard
to find the right words
and harder
to say them out loud
and hardest
of all
to see
what each word did
to Mom and Dad.

But I kept
going.

I told them

about Nick Fisher
what he said
in that hallway
in fourth grade
how he spat it
in front of everyone
and how I came home
and ruined my clothes
and started hiding
in hoodies
and hiding
so much else
and how Dave
and Andrew
and Devin—
how we drifted
apart
and how it left me
alone
and lonely
and sad
and eating
to stop feeling
so sad
but how that
just made me
feel worse

because eating—
the way
I was eating
was part of
the problem—
but I didn't—
I couldn't—
I didn't know
what to do
so I'd reach
for more food
to push away
the sadness
but of course
it came back
so I ate
and ate
and ate
and not eating
was my way
to stop
the whole cycle
and fix
the problem
at the center
of it all:

ME.

I said
all that
then got up
and went
to the bathroom.
I blew my nose.
I wiped my eyes.
I peed.
Then I went back
and sat down
right where I'd been.

I felt

    nervous.

A little scared.

Ashamed.

My heart
was beating
fast
and hard.

But beneath
all that—

mixed in with
those not-so-great
emotions—
I felt

    relief.

It was like ...

    like I'd been sitting
    in a burning building
    for the past
    few years
    and I'd finally called
    for help.

So I went on
sitting there.
I let
my parents
ask questions—

    so many questions.

I let them
try
to help.

I was upstairs
back in bed
exhausted
from talking
and needing
a break
when I heard
the knock.

And I knew—
somehow
I just knew
who it was.

I heard Mom
go to the door
and heard her
talking to him
and then heard her
call up to me.

And I almost
didn't answer.
I almost
pretended
that I'd gone back
to sleep.

I almost
hid up there
in my bedroom
like I'd been hiding
for years.

Almost . . .

But then
I got up.
I got
out of bed
and took
one step
  after another
            down
          the hall
              down
              the stairs
                  toward
                  the open
                  door.

He was out front
with a skateboard tucked
beneath each arm.

Markus.

Black jeans.

Black T-shirt.

Neon-green
fingernails.

He looked
right at me
and didn't
look away.

I tried
to do
the same.

"Hey,"
he said.

And I said,
"Hey."

I put on some shoes
and went outside
met Markus
on the curb
at the edge of
the lawn.

"This is
for you
by the way,"
he told me
patting one
of the two skateboards
lying on the grass
beside him.

"For . . .
What?
You're joking."

Markus turned
to face me.
Brushed the hair
away from his eyes
so he could see me
when he said,
"I've never been

more serious
about anything
in my life."

"I can't
skateboard."

"Probably because
you've never tried."

"No.
I mean . . .
I'm—"

"Get up."

"Huh?"

Markus stood up
all of a sudden
grabbing both boards
as he did.

"Get up."

He set the boards
on the street

then pointed at one
like he wanted me
to get on.

And secretly
a part of me
had been wanting
to do this—
to try
to skateboard.
Watching Markus
it was hard
not to.
But that
didn't mean
I thought
I actually
COULD.

But I could tell
Markus wasn't gonna stop
until this happened.

So . . .

I got up
and put one foot

on the board.
Markus did
too
keeping it steady
and leaning in
so I could set
my hands
on his shoulders
and get
my other foot
up on the board
as well.

It was weird—
touching him
holding on to him
standing there
with our faces
just a few inches
apart.

But I didn't
have long
to worry about
any of that.

Because two seconds after

I'd grabbed on to him
Markus said,
"Now I'm gonna
take my foot off."

"What?
No.
You're—
don't."

"You're gonna wobble a bit.
But you're gonna bend
your knees
and put your arms out
and balance.
You're gonna find
your balance.
Okay?
Ready?"

"No!
I'm—"

He took his foot off
and stepped away
and I wobbled
just like he said.

I wobbled
like crazy.
But I bent my knees
and threw my arms out
just like he said
and even though
I was sure
I was about to fall
and break my arm
or crack my head open
I didn't
and actually
I did it—
I found it—
my balance.

"Now I'm gonna give you
a push."

"WHAT?!"

"I'm gonna push you along
and I'm gonna hold on
for a minute
but then
I'm gonna let go."

And suddenly—

    all of
        a sudden

—I was rolling.

Slowly.

But then
less slowly.

And then
less slowly
still.

And then—

Markus took one hand
off my shoulder
and the other one
off my back
and I was still
rolling
still
riding
still

hurtling forward
all on
my own
with air
in my hair
and a whoosh
in my ears—
terrified and
ecstatic and
pretty sure
I was gonna
hurt myself
any second
but feeling like
I never
ever
wanted
to stop.

————————————————

"We're gonna
make a deal
okay?
I'm gonna
teach you
how to skate
and you'll

show me
how to draw.
And don't say
you can't.
Don't pretend
you're not awesome
at drawing.
I've seen
enough.
You're good.
Crazy
good.
And I want
to get better.
So . . .
okay?
Sound
good?
Do we have
a deal?"

"Deal."

"Can I ask you
something?
I think

I know
what you're gonna
say—
but can I ask you
anyway?"

"Shoot."

"Why
are you here?"

That's all
I said
because I knew
Markus knew
what I meant.

I knew he knew
that I was mentioning
without mentioning
all the ways
I'd pushed him away
before actually
physically
in that hallway
the other day
pushing him

away.
Mentioning
all that
and asking
why the heck
he was back
giving me
another
chance.

"I guess . . .
Well
I mean
I could tell
I liked you.
You know how
there's some people
and when you first meet them
you just **KNOW**?
It was like
that.
I knew
that you—
drawing out back
behind the auditorium
all on your own—
I thought that

315

was cool.
And I just knew
that you
were someone
I wanted to know
more about.
And you kept
making it hard
yeah.
But I think—
I guess
I'm the type of person
who that sort of thing
doesn't work on.
It just made me
want to know about you
even more.
Does that make
any sense?"

"Yeah,"
I told him.
"It does."

Not really the part
about me being alone
being cool.

I still don't quite
get that.
But what he said
about how
you can meet someone
and just KNOW—

in your body
in your bones

—that they're someone
you want
in your life—

that's exactly
how I felt
about him.

"Okay.
You asked me something.
So now can I
tell you something?
Can I tell you
what I didn't finish
telling you
last week?"

His story.

The rest of
his story.

"The way I
look at it—
the way
I think
about myself
is like
a work in progress.
Have you heard that
before?
That
phrase?
I learned about it
at one of my fifty-seven
middle schools.
In an art class.
My teacher—
she showed us
these paintings.
There were
a bunch of them.
They were all
by different painters

but they were all
portraits.
You know.
Of other people.
And they were all
just . . .
not finished.
In one
the whole bottom half
of the canvas
was totally blank.
In another
the guy's face
was painted
but the rest of his body
was only outlined
in black.
And my teacher—
she said
she didn't know
if those painters
meant to finish
their portraits
or if they left them
in progress
on purpose.
But she said

she liked to think
it **HAD** been
on purpose—
that all those artists
had wanted
to make a point
about how it's impossible
to capture a person
on canvas
when they're always changing—
always becoming
different people
even if only
little by little—
right
before
your eyes.
And I didn't think of it
right then.
But it wasn't too long
after.
I thought,
That's it.
That's what
I am
too.
That's what

I feel like
so often.
A work
in progress.
Not finished.
Not yet.
Never finished.
Always changing
whether I like it
or not
and always having
to catch up
with myself.
Because every day
something else is happening
to me.
I'm thinking
and feeling
new
and different
things.
And that—
if you look at it
the right way
there's something
amazing in that.
Something really . . .

powerful.
Something
FREEING.
Thinking of myself
as unfinished
in that way—
it's gotten me to be
a lot kinder
to myself.
You know?
It's helped me see
all the awesome stuff
about me
even though
I'm also more aware
of some stuff
I might want
to be different.
I'm just
more okay
with **ME**—
even if
I come across
a super-unfinished
part of me.
I mean
all I can do

is wake up
every day
and **BE** me.
So I might as well
try
to be as me
as I can be.
And the more me
I am?
The more
I try
every day
to be as me
as I can
possibly be
the better
I feel.
The happier
I am.
So that's
what I do.
Just keep trying
to paint a picture
that's as real
and true
as can be.
Knowing that tomorrow

I'll want
to change this
and I'll have
to add that.
And also knowing
that there's no
work of art
that everyone in the world
is gonna love.
But somewhere out there—
you've got to believe
that somewhere out there
there are people
who are gonna
appreciate it.
Who are gonna
appreciate
YOU."

I went upstairs
as soon as Markus left.

I went upstairs
and into
the bathroom
and stood
in front of
the mirror.

I took off
my sweatshirt.

I took off
my T-shirt.

And I looked.

I looked
and looked
and looked.

I saw
a kid
who couldn't
stop eating.
I saw

a kid
who needed
to not eat
ever again.
I saw
a kid
who girls
would never kiss
and guys
would never want
to be around.
I saw
a monster.

But I tried—

    I looked
    and I looked
    and I tried—

to see
the me
that Markus saw
when he looked
at me.

A kid

who was different
in a good way—
a COOL way.
A kid
who was good
at drawing.
A kid
who had just
gone skateboarding
for the very first time.
A kid
worth hanging out with
even when
he made hanging out with him
super hard.
A kid
who someone
appreciated—

and someone
who the kid appreciated
right back.

I tried
to see
all that
and I . . .

I couldn't.

Not really.

It was hard.

But
I went on standing there.

I stared
into the mirror
and I tried
and tried
and tried.

My parents
made me two
appointments.

The first
is with
my doctor—
the one
I've been seeing
since I was
a baby.

The other
is with
a therapist.
This woman
I've never met
but talked to
for a while
on the phone.

Marci.

That's
her name.
And that's what
she told me

to call her.

She sounded
nice enough.
And young
too.
Not at all
like the serious
cold old lady
I imagined
before Dad
handed me the phone.

She asked me
about myself.
And I started telling her
all the stuff
I'd told Mom and Dad—
about being humiliated
in a crowded hallway
in fourth grade
and about destroying
all my clothes.
But before
I could get
too far
she stopped me.

She asked me
to tell her
what I liked
to do.

And so we talked
about drawing.
We talked
about my favorite comics
and graphic novels—
a couple of which
she'd actually read
because her niece
is a big reader
and last summer
they formed their own
two-person book club.
We talked
about skateboarding
and I told her
about Markus
and an hour passed
and then almost half
of another
and I was actually bummed
when she said
she had to go.

"But,"
she told me,
"we'll talk again
soon.
Can we?
Would you like
to come talk with me
every week?"

I told her
I did.
I told her
that sounded
great.

And it really
did.

Markus
is moving.

AGAIN.

He's moving
to a town
two thousand miles
away.

It's been
three weeks
since he gave me
that skateboard.
Three weeks
since we
started hanging out—

like
ACTUALLY
hanging out

—and now . . .

he's leaving.

I want

to cry.

Maybe
I already did cry
a little bit.

But it's
okay.

It's gonna be
okay.

At least
that's what Markus
says.

And Mom and Dad
and Marci
too.

Markus says
his parents
are getting him
a phone.
We'll talk.
He'll text me pics
of his drawings

and I'll—

"You better,"
he warns me.

—send him videos
of me skating.

He says
it's not like
we'll never talk
or see each other
again.

It's okay.

That's what
I'm telling myself now.

It's gonna be
okay.

I'm wearing shorts
and a T-shirt.
No hoodie.
No baggy jeans.

It took me twenty minutes
to psych myself up enough
to leave the house
wearing it.

But here I am
leaving behind
the already hot day
and stepping into
school—

    stepping into
    a hallway
    filled with
    other kids.

I move slow.
Hang around
in the area
I know
she'll be passing through
soon.

And soon
enough . . .

　　it happens.

There
she is—

　　Jules

—heading
down the hallway
toward me.

And I feel
how I always feel
when I see her.

Like I want
to run
but also
stay
and look
at her
and talk
to her—
ask her

all sorts
of questions
and hear
all her answers.

You can do it.

You can do this.

I hope so.
I've practiced it
a million times
in my head
and even
out loud
in front of
the mirror.

I wait
till she's
a little
closer.

And then . . .

I smile.

Nothing
too big.
Just a little
lift of
my lips.

And then—

    she's close now
    only a handful of steps
    away

—I open my mouth
and say,

    "Hey."

It takes her
a second
to realize
I'm talking
to her.

Then

    she stops.
    So do

her friends.

"Hey . . . ,"
I say.

You already
said that part,
Will.

". . . Jules."

Why are her eyes
so wide?

What's going on
with her eyes?

Why won't she
blink?

Blink.

Blink!

Please
blink.

She blinks.
"Oh,"
she says.
"Hi, Will.
It's—"

She puts a hand
to her lips.

"It's Will
right?"

"Yeah."

Okay.
Now hurry up.

Don't make her
STAND there.

"Drawing."

That's what
I say.

Jules looks
confused.

Which makes
total sense.

Come **ON**,
Will.

"I—
I mean—
I know—
well, I think—
I'm pretty sure
you like
to draw
and me—
I . . .
I draw
too."

One of Jules's friends
snorts.

The other
just looks horrified.

But I just
keep looking
at Jules.

And she—
—she smiles.

Nothing
too big.

Just a little
lift of
her lips.

But I can tell
it's the good
kind of smile.
Not her
on the verge of laughing
at me
but her
made happy
just by the thought
of drawing.

"I think—
I might . . .
I may
start a club?"

One of Jules's friends

mutters, "Oh my GOSH."
But Jules—
she smiles
bigger
and then says,
"Yeah?"

"Yes.
Yeah.
I'm going
to start
a drawing club.
It won't be—
it'll start up
next year.
But I don't—
maybe—
I don't know . . ."

Just spit it out,
Will.
You're almost there.

"I just—
I wanted
to let you know
in case

you maybe
wanted
to join."

THERE.

"Yeah,"
she says.
"Maybe.
I might.
That could be
really cool
actually."

"Yeah . . . ,"
I say.

And a part of me
wants to go on standing there
a little longer
wants to ask her
about her favorite books
and about what sketchbooks
she uses
and where she gets
her pencils
and markers

and if she prefers
drawing with one
over the other.

But I think
that maybe
this won't be
the last conversation
Jules and I have.

Hopefully
I get a chance
to ask her
all of that
another time.

So I just
give her a nod.
Another
little smile.

Then
    I go.

I keep

    walking.

Down

the hall

and on with

my day.

I'm not
very good
at skateboarding.

I kind of
actually—

definitely

—suck.

And no—
I'm **NOT**
being extra hard
on myself.

Even Markus
says I suck.

But he also says,

"I sucked
at first
too."

He says,

"Most people suck
at stuff they've never tried
before."

He says,

"Every day you skate
you're gonna suck
a little less."

And I guess
that's what
it's all about.

Getting up
and trying.
Trying
and trying
and trying
again.
Trying—
and ending
the day
sucking a little less
than you started.

Every day
I wake up
and remind myself
of certain things.

Things my parents
told me.
And my doctor
told me.
And Marci
keeps telling me
every time
it comes up
in our sessions.

not bad
NOT bad

Like that food
isn't bad.
And eating
isn't bad.
And the size
and shape
of my body
aren't bad.

Some people might
think differently.
They might think that way

without even knowing it.

But it's not
my job
to change the way
everyone else
thinks
and feels.

It's not
my job
to bend
and twist
and contort
myself
to make other people
more comfortable
and happy.

And I can't
just magically change
what everyone else
thinks
and feels
when they see
me.

All I can do—

> what I need
> to do

—is work on changing
what I think
and feel
when I see
me.

Because that—
THAT
is what
the problem
has been
all along.

Not
my body.

Not the size
of my stomach
or how
and when
I get hungry.

But the shame
and hate
that come with it
and that spiraled
        out of control
and consumed me.

If I change that—

        if I work
        on changing
        that

—I think—
I hope—
I have to
believe
that everything else
will start
to get better
too.

I still
have days
when I want
to hide
in a hoodie.
Days
when I don't
even want
to get out
of bed.
Days
when I feel
like a monster.
When I look
at myself
and feel hate
and shame
and rage.
Days
when I eat
more than I need
and feel terrible
about it.

But mixed in
with the bad days
are okay ones.

Sometimes
even good ones.
Days when I barely
even think about
my body
and how much
I'm eating.
Or days when I do
and feel okay
about all of it.

And I think
that's how it is
for everyone.
That mix
of bad and good
and okay.

I think
that's just
being human.

And I think
we've all got crap
we're dealing with.

We're all

works in progress.

I know
I am.

And I'm just trying
to have as many good days
and okay days
as I can.
And trying
not to beat myself up
when I don't.

I'm just

    trying
               to find
      some balance.

Like I do
on my skateboard.

Sometimes
I tip one way
or the other.

Sometimes

I straight-up
fall down.

But I always
get back up.

I always
get back on.

I plant
my feet
and push.

I push
and push

    onward.

      Forward.

        Ahead.

Trying

and failing

but trying

again . . .

RESOURCES

Some organizations working to improve the
lives of people suffering from mental illness
are listed below. This listing is being provided
for informational purposes only and is not
intended to be either an endorsement or
promotion of any listed organization, nor
does it imply that such organizations have
been endorsed by the author or publisher.
It is also not intended to be a complete or
exhaustive listing or a substitute for the
advice of a qualified medical or mental health
professional.

childmind.org/topics/eating-eating-disorders

nationaleatingdisorders.org

aedweb.org/resources/about-eating-disorders

ACKNOWLEDGMENTS

Thank you to Myrsini Stephanides for encouraging me to write this story the second she heard about it and for supporting me every step of the way.

Thank you to Karen Nagel for taking this project on and for pushing me—with the utmost care and respect—to do what I needed to do to get it right.

Thank you to Heather Palisi for her sharp eye, brilliant ideas, and devotion to detail.

Thank you to Megan Gendell for the precision and care with which she attended to every single word (and period and comma!) of this story.

Thank you to everyone else at Simon & Schuster and Aladdin who had a hand in helping this book become what it is and everyone who's out there now helping make sure it reaches as many readers as possible.

Thank you to Isla, River, and Soleia for being exactly who you are.

Thank you, as always, to Danni—for every single thing.

And thank you to you—yes, YOU—for reading this.

ABOUT THE AUTHOR

Jarrett Lerner is the award-winning creator of more than a dozen books for kids, including the Enginerds series of middle-grade novels, the Geeger the Robot series of early chapter books, the Hunger Heroes series of graphic novel chapter books, two activity books, and the Nat the Cat series of early readers. You can find him online at jarrettlerner.com and on Twitter and Instagram at @Jarrett_Lerner. He lives with his wife and daughters in Massachusetts.